The Karate Way

*To Nicholas,
I hope you enjoy my book!
Osu!
2001*

Written and illustrated by Sensei Gary Hellman

A Doubleday Book for Young Readers

A special thank-you to Candice Chaplin

A Doubleday Book for Young Readers
Published by
Random House Children's Books
a division of
Random House, Inc.
1540 Broadway
New York, New York 10036
Doubleday and the anchor with dolphin colophon are registered trademarks of
Random House, Inc.

Visit us on the Web! www.randomhouse.com/kids
Educators and librarians, for a variety of teaching tools, visit us at www.randomhouse.com/teachers

Cataloging-in-Publication Data is available from the U.S. Library of Congress.
ISBN: 0-385-32742-0

The text of this book is set in 16-point Goudy.

Book design by Patrice Sheridan

Manufactured in the United States of America

April 2001

10 9 8 7 6 5 4 3 2 1

This book is dedicated to Master Tiger Schulmann,
my teacher and friend,
and the rest of my extended T.S.K. family and students.

To my inspirational wife, Bubba;
Stevie, my son, whom the star of this book is modeled after;
and my beautiful daughter, Amanda the panda.

Anyone out there who would like to get in touch and exchange ideas
can reach me at www.tsk.com.

The story I'm about to tell you is true. Last September I was sitting on the steps of my house with my dog, Sir Marlowe. I'd been thinking about the terrible day I'd just had. "Killer Miller" was my new teacher, the toughest teacher in my grade. Some bully had shot a spitball in my ear. And my parents were going to sign me up for an after-school activity the next day.

They wouldn't tell me what it was. They said it was a surprise. I had never liked surprises. It was not a good day at all. I was worried.

I worried all night.

I hoped it wasn't football. I wasn't very strong.

I hoped it wasn't tennis. I wasn't fast enough.

I hoped it wasn't basketball. I was too short.

The next day after school, my mom drove me to my new activity. Mom was one smart cookie, because if I had known she was taking me to a karate school, I never would have gotten out of the car. I tried to escape, but Mom was strong as well as smart. She said, "Give it a try. We're not leaving until you meet your teacher."

I had no choice, so I closed my eyes and waited to be karate-chopped in half.

When I opened my eyes, the teacher was standing there.
He was big, but he had an even bigger smile. Maybe this wasn't
going to be so bad after all.

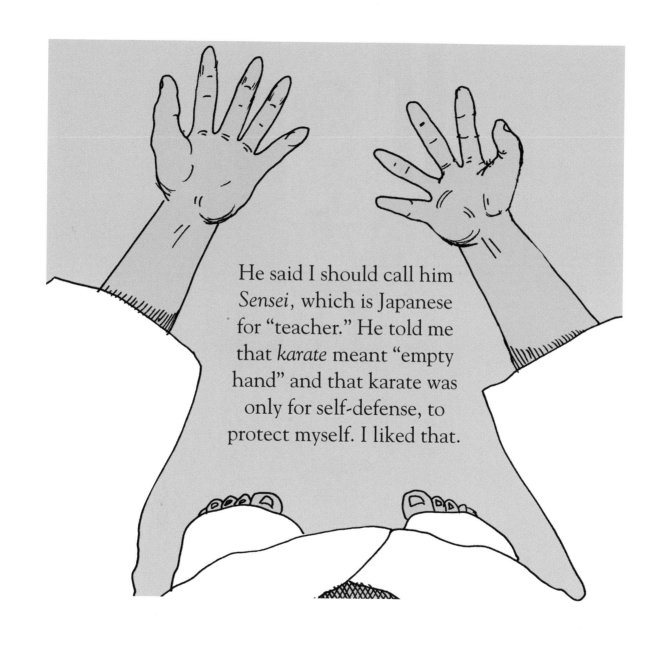

He said I should call him *Sensei*, which is Japanese for "teacher." He told me that *karate* meant "empty hand" and that karate was only for self-defense, to protect myself. I liked that.

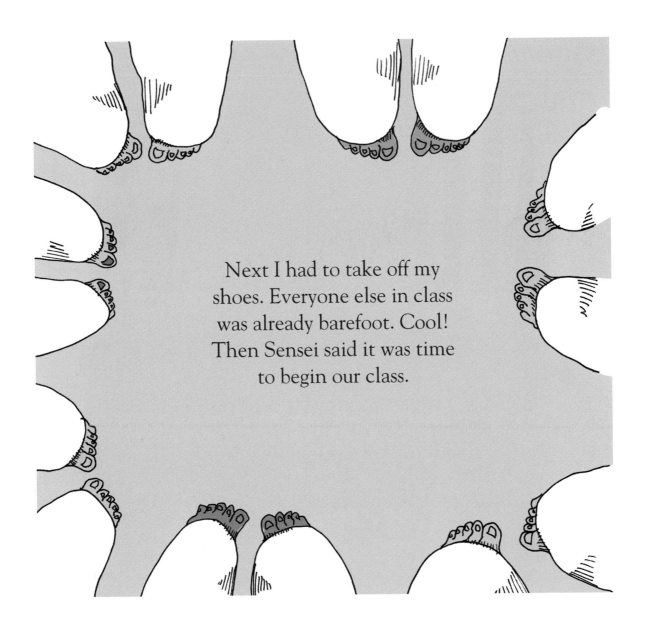

Next I had to take off my
shoes. Everyone else in class
was already barefoot. Cool!
Then Sensei said it was time
to begin our class.

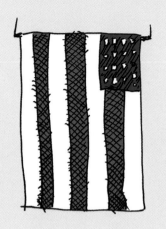

Bowing is for saying hello and goodbye.
Saying *"Osu"* means "Yes, I understand."

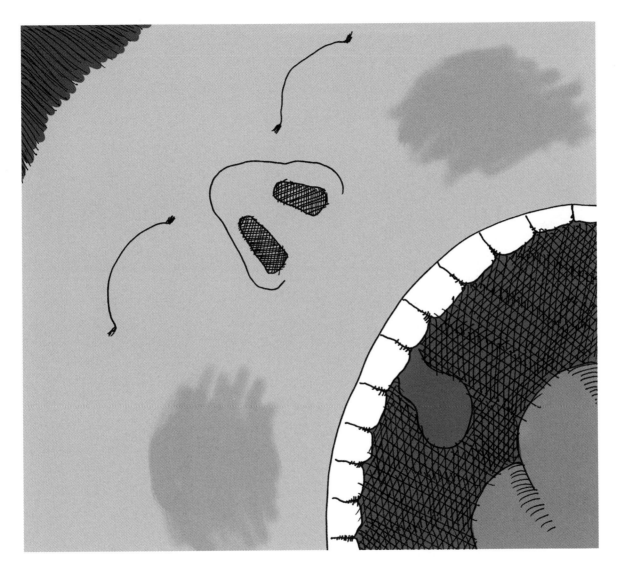

The wider you open your mouth, the louder you can yell.
A loud karate shout is called *kiai* and is for scaring away bullies
and giving you more power. *E-E-E-YA!!!*

I did karate for one hour straight. It was so much fun that it felt like five minutes! After class Mom bought me a uniform called a *gi*. It was a little too big at first, but she promised to sew it right away so I could practice that night.

When we got home Mom gave me a Popsicle. It reminded me of our attention stance in karate. We had to be frozen with our hands at our sides, feet together, and eyes straight ahead. Sensei said this would help us concentrate so we could learn faster, not only in karate but in school too. It works!

I went to karate class after school a few days a week. After class, Sir Marlowe always helped me practice. We worked on my defensive stance. I turned sideways so he couldn't hit me in the stomach, and I kept my hands up to protect my face.

It was easy to practice my balance because Sir Marlowe likes to jump on me and lick me.

Out of all the kicks I learned, the round kick was my favorite.
You have to pick your leg up and stick it out to the side like a table.
Then you snap the bottom part of your leg out and back. I liked
this kick because while I practiced I could have milk and cookies.

After practicing, Sir Marlowe and I always stretched. We made sure we were sweaty first so we wouldn't pull a muscle. I loved karate class! I practiced every day.

I can hardly believe it! It's been six months since I started karate. I just got my blue belt in today's class. There are many different-colored belts. You earn each one as you get better, and at each belt you learn a different self-defense move and a different kick. One day I want to be a black belt. That's the best one.

I've made lots of friends in class, like Brittney, Brian, Troy, and Kyle. We practice together before and after class. It makes me feel good to know I can defend myself if I have to.

I used the concentration I learned in karate to get good grades in Killer Miller's class. Now Mom says I can take an extra activity this year!

Maybe I'll take football. I've gotten stronger from kicking and punching.

Maybe I'll take tennis. I think I could hit the cover off the ball!

Maybe I'll take basketball. I'm not much taller than last year, but now that I know how to defend myself, I feel I'm as big as anyone.

It sure is great not to worry so much. Karate taught me how to feel good about myself and have a non-quitting spirit. I feel like I can do anything now, as long as I work hard and don't give up. I'm glad my mom made me try it. Thanks, Mom!

Order of Karate Belts

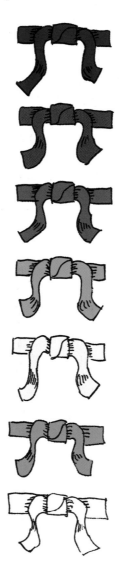

Glossary

Dojo
The place where karate is practiced

Gi
The karate uniform

Karate
Kara (empty) + *Te* (hand) = *Karate*, literally "empty hand"; because in karate, no weapons are used

Karateka
A person who practices karate

Kiai
A karate shout that helps focus energy into movement; literally, "the blending of inner spirit with physical strength"

Osu
Hello; Goodbye; Yes, I understand.

Sensei
Sen (before) + *Sei* (born) = *Sensei*, literally "born before"; karate teacher

About the Author

Gary Hellman has been training in the martial arts for over twenty-five years. He is currently the head instructor at Tiger Schulmann's Karate in Clearwater, Florida. Gary is known as Sensei to his students and holds a fifth-degree black belt. He still actively trains under the direction of Master Danny "Tiger" Schulmann and has passed his knowledge on to thousands of students of his own.

Sensei Hellman lives in Clearwater with his wife, Denise, and their two children, Steven and Amanda.